PUFFIN BOOKS

The Last Polar Bears

Roo lives with Harry Horse and Mandy in an old farmhouse in the Scottish Borders. She has turned down several film offers since the publication of *The Last Polar Bears*, preferring instead to concentrate on rabbits. It is her ambition to own one eventually. She is currently working on her first book, provisionally entitled *The Bad Rabbits*.

Harry Horse writes and illustrates children's books. His titles include *The Last Gold Diggers*, for which he won the Smarties Gold Award. He is well known as a political cartoonist and has produced cartoons for the *New Yorker*, the *Guardian* and the *Sunday Herald*. Unusually, rabbits do not play a large part in his life.

Some other books by Harry Horse

THE LAST CASTAWAYS
THE LAST COWBOYS
THE LAST GOLD DIGGERS

The Last Polar Bears

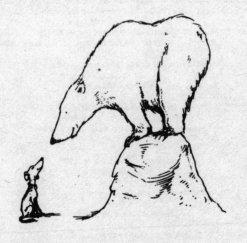

Written and illustrated by Harry Horse

PUFFIN BOOKS

After publication of this book, it was pointed out to me that it bears some resemblance to Mervyn Peake's *Letters from a Lost Uncle*. I should like to point out that although I greatly admire Mervyn Peake's work, any similarities are purely coincidental, my inspiration being members of my family, in particular my grandfather and my dog Roo.

– Harry Horse

PUFFIN BOOKS

Published by the Penguin Group
Penguin Books Ltd, 80 Strand, London WC2R 0RL, England
Penguin Putnam Inc., 375 Hudson Street, New York, New York 10014, USA
Penguin Books Australia Ltd, 250 Camberwell Road, Camberwell, Victoria 3124, Australia
Penguin Books Canada Ltd, 10 Alcorn Avenue, Toronto, Ontario, Canada M4V 3B2
Penguin Books India (P) Ltd, 11 Community Centre, Panchsheel Park,
New Delhi – 110 017, India
Penguin Books (NZ) Ltd, Cnr Rosedale and Airborne Roads, Albany, Auckland, New Zealand
Penguin Books (South Africa) (Pty) Ltd, 24 Sturdee Avenue, Rosebank 2196, South Africa

Penguin Books Ltd, Registered Offices: 80 Strand, London WC2R 0RL, England

www.penguin.com

First published by Viking 1993
Published in Puffin Books 1996
This edition published for World Book Day 2003
1

Filmset in American Typewriter

Printed in England by Clays Ltd, St Ives plc

British Library Cataloguing in Publication Data
A CIP catalogue record for this book is available from the British Library

ISBN 0-141-31654-3

The Official Map
of
~ WALRUS ~
Population: 17½

Scale: |⊢━━ This Much ━━⊣| = Quite a long way

Dear Child,

I am writing to let you know that Roo and I are well. I'm sorry that I was unable to say goodbye to you properly and I hope that you can understand why I had to go on this expedition. I am going to the North Pole to find the Last Polar Bears. I have to see them as they really are. I want to see them swimming amongst the icebergs and playing in the snow.

You see, I remember going to the zoo one hot summer's afternoon and seeing my first polar bear.

He was sitting in the shade of a dead tree. There was a small concrete pool for him to swim in. The water was green. I looked at the polar bear. There was no snow for him to roll in, no icebergs for him to float upon . . . That was no life for a polar bear!

I could not save him. How could I? You can hardly smuggle a polar bear under your coat and walk out with him, can you?

That day, I decided to go to the North Pole to see how the polar bears really live. I went to the library and I read everything I could find

Roo did this! This page is ruined!

about polar bears: where they live, what they eat, and how to look for them in remote places. I studied many maps until one day, in the British Museum, I found the map of Great Bear Ridge, and I knew then that that is where I would find the Last Polar Bears.

I began to plan an expedition. Your mother said I was too old to go off to the North Pole by myself, but all my life I have either been too old or too young to do what I wanted to do, so this time I decided that I would listen to no one. I booked my passage on the good ship *Unsinkable*.

I decided, after a lot of thought, to take Roo with me. Huskies would be better, but I couldn't afford to feed them. Roo said that her particular breed were in fact better than huskies but that no one had ever given them the chance to prove it. When I told her that our expedition was to the North Pole she said she had heard of it, and that one of her relations helped to put it up.

We sneaked out of the house one night whilst you were fast asleep. I didn't wake you, for you know I hate to say goodbye. I took your Uncle Freddie's golf trolley to use as our sledge. Tell him I only want it for a little while.

Tell your mother I'm sorry, but I had to go.

Don't worry, I'll be back.

With love,

your Grandfather.

Dear Child,

I have a very nice cabin. It has two portholes: one for
Roo, and one for me.

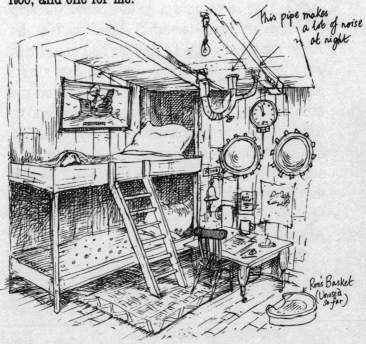

This pipe makes
a lot of noise
at night

Roo's Basket
(Unused
so far)

So far I have seen a lot of seagulls and a porpoise. Roo
said she saw a sheep.

Roo has not been a very good sailor. She says that
dogs aren't supposed to go on boats. I told her that

some boats always have a cat on board, to kill rats. Roo said that anything a cat can do, a dog can do better, and that dogs are famous for being great sailors. She said that her grandfather was probably the captain of a ship – and that he probably killed hundreds of rats. 'He probably did,' I said.

This afternoon Roo asked the captain if she could have a go at steering the ship. 'Dogs are great steerers of ships,' she told him. He let her have a little go, and for half an hour we went around in circles. Roo said that dogs always steer ships in this way. The captain was worried about the ship hitting a rock, so he took over and we continued in a straight line towards the North Pole.

I am giving these letters to some fishermen who are on their way back home to Aberdeen. They said they had seen some bad storms, with waves as big as houses. I must finish this letter now as they are getting ready to sail away.

Will write again soon,

With love,

your Grandfather.

Dear Child,

We have been at sea for almost a week now. Every
day Roo asks if we are there yet, and every day I have
to say, 'Not yet, but soon, very soon.' It is a long way
to the North Pole and I need to keep her spirits up.
The sea is such a big place. It seems to go on for ever.
We did see some land yesterday. The captain pointed
out the islands of Shetland, but he didn't stop as he
said we had to make good time if we wanted to reach
the North Pole before the bad weather. Of course, I
never mentioned anything about bad weather to Roo,
as I thought it might upset her. She has been rather a
nuisance I'm afraid, and I begin to wonder whether it
was such a good idea to bring her along in the first
place. I thought she might be
useful pulling the trolley up
the steep bits. Perhaps I
should have brought a
husky after all.

Today Roo announced
that she had changed
her mind about finding
the Last Polar Bears and
that she had decided to go

home. She said that she had been mistaken and it isn't snow that her particular breed are good on, it is sand. I said it was impossible to turn around and go back now and that we just had to press on. Roo said that dogs are excellent swimmers and that she could swim back if she wanted to. I had to put her lead on and tie her to the mast as I was frightened that she just might try it. She howled all afternoon until I untied her.

Tonight Roo insisted on sleeping in a hammock. I didn't think this was a very good idea, but she said that her grandfather had probably slept in one all the time he was at sea. I finally agreed, but I warned her not to stand up in the hammock. She ignored me completely and promptly fell out on to the floor. I wish she would sleep in her basket like a normal dog. She is now in my bed, which is very uncomfortable for me. The boat is going up and down and I have spilt ink all over the sheets.

Feeling a little poorly.

Your Grandfather...

Dear Child,

What a horrible night! I don't think I slept a wink. Roo pulled all the covers off me and wrapped herself in a ball at my feet. The boat was leaping around all night and twice I ended up on the floor. I can't remember anything else, but when I woke up this morning I was in Roo's basket at the foot of the bed.

The captain cooked a hearty breakfast of sausages, bacon and eggs, but I couldn't eat a scrap, I felt so sick. I just had to sit there and watch Roo and the captain wolf down the lot. Roo, her mouth full of toast and marmalade, explained between bites how dogs never suffer from seasickness on account of them having four legs. Having four legs means you never wobble about, explained Roo, and she then went on to tell the captain the most ridiculous story about her grandfather, saying that he had been in a storm so bad that he had spent the whole voyage upside-down, and that in the end he got quite used to it, and that he even preferred it to being the right way up. After that, she said, he always had his dinner standing on his head.

I don't object to Roo telling tall stories, but I *do* object to her changing her mind. At breakfast she told the captain that it had always been her ambition to see the North Pole, yet this afternoon she said that she couldn't care less about some stupid old pole, and she didn't want to see any polar bears either. She has been in a bad mood all day and things are even worse now she has lost her red ball. She was playing run and catch by herself on the deck when it rolled overboard and was eaten by a passing shark.

Very sleepy tonight. I have not had breakfast, lunch or tea today. Will send this letter as soon as I can. Roo is in her basket and I am going to bed. Very rough seas tonight. The ship is making horrible groaning noises. Can't write any more.

your Grandfather.

Monday 14 October
Somewhere near Iceland,
but not sure exactly where
On board the *Unthankable*

Dear Child,

We have now been on our expedition for
ten days. Of course we are not there yet,
but at least we are on our way. Once we get
there we can begin to practise climbing
and looking for the best route up to Great
Bear Ridge. I have never been on an expedition
before and neither has Roo, but I know that you can't
hurry. We have to be careful. Terrible things can
happen on an expedition if you hurry. You could fall
down a crevasse, or get lost in a snowstorm. I intend
to do a lot of planning so that things like that won't
happen to Roo and me.

Roo said she wouldn't have come along if she had
known it was going to be *that* type of expedition, and
that she thought we were just going away for a couple
of days. I tried to explain that expeditions *always* take
a long time. If they only lasted a couple of days then
everyone would go on one. It isn't like going to the
beach for a picnic. You can't come home at night for
your tea.

All this talk of beaches and picnics put me in
rather a sorry mood and I suddenly missed you all,

even Uncle Freddie. I went out on deck. The sun was setting. A gentle wind blew overhead. I wondered whether I was wrong to have come all this way. Maybe the polar bears wouldn't want to see us. Maybe we would get lost in a snowstorm. Maybe . . . My thoughts were interrupted by the captain shouting at me to batten down the hatches and lash down any loose barrels. I didn't see the hurry. The sea looked so calm. 'The calm before the storm,' whispered the captain. A minute later there was a growl of thunder and huge black clouds rolled in overhead.

'Get below!' ordered the captain, after I had finished all the battening and lashing. I looked at the sea. It seemed angry. I quickly went below into the cabin as I didn't want to make it any angrier.

We did not talk much this evening as we ate our supper. I had to hold on to my plate to stop it sliding off the table. The captain said nothing, though he roared with laughter every time a large wave struck the boat. He drank rather a lot of rum tonight, I'm afraid. He fell asleep in his chair. Roo said that she would steer if I wanted, but I thought it would be safer for both of us to get into bed. We pulled the covers up over our heads, but it didn't keep the noise of the storm out.

Another sleepless night ahead. Do not worry, I am used to it.

With love,

your Grandfather.

My dear Child,

I was woken in the middle of the night by Roo barking that the ship was sinking. At first I just grabbed my dressing-gown, but I didn't want to be marooned at sea in my night-clothes, so I tried to get dressed over my pyjamas. I could hardly pull my trousers on, the boat was lurching about so much. Water was pouring in under the door, the cupboards were swinging open, and all my clothes, maps and equipment lay strewn across the floor in a soggy heap. Roo was running round in circles, with a rubber-ring around her middle. I managed to get the cabin door open and we struggled out into the corridor, where we met the captain. He seemed quite unconcerned about the storm and asked us what we were doing. Roo gibbered something about lifeboats and every dog for itself, until the captain wrapped her in an oilskin blanket and popped her in the boot locker for her own protection. He then sent me back to bed with some tea that tasted strongly of rum.

This morning the storm finally died away.

The captain, who had tied me to the bed so that I wouldn't fall out, untied me and let Roo out of the boot locker. I bore him no grudge, but Roo sulked and said she didn't feel like breakfast. She only ate five rashers of bacon, three poached eggs and seven slices of toast.

I went to our cabin, began to tidy up the mess and spent most of the morning folding, sorting and drying. When I had finished, Roo poked her nose round the door and asked if she could lend a paw. I feel very alone on this expedition and know that I shall probably end up doing all the work myself.

After lunch the captain began work on the engine. It seems that last night it took a bit of a pounding from the storm. I'm not an engineer, but I went down to the engine-room with him to see if I could help. I told Roo to stay up on deck and not get into any trouble.

The engine looked a bit of a mess. Oil was dripping from the pipes, and a lot of cogs, nuts and bolts seemed to have sprung loose. I picked up as many as I could find and the captain put them back into the engine. For many hours he worked inside the engine, sometimes crawling in so far that only his feet poked out. At last the final bolt was put back in its place, and after the captain had done a bit more adjusting, he tried to start the engine. He pressed the starter-motor. Nothing happened. He pressed the emergency starter-motor. Nothing. Then he whacked it with his spanner. Still it wouldn't start. He even booted it with his foot. At that moment Roo came down the ladder, tripped, and fell on to some buttons. The engine roared into life. The captain was amazed and said that it had never sounded better.

Roo said that her uncle had lived in a garage and that's how she knew so much about engines. I said I had never heard of an engineer-dog. Roo said that if there were police-dogs, guard-dogs, guide-dogs, sheep-dogs and rescue-dogs, then there were bound to be engineer-dogs and possibly doctor-dogs as well.

A hearty meal tonight, and even the captain in a good mood for once. We all had a game of Old Maid. Roo won nineteen games in a row.

Very sleepy, will write more tomorrow.

your Grandfather

Thursday 17 October
Somewhere near the North Pole
On board the *Unsingable*

Dear Child,

So much happened yesterday that I was unable to sit down and write you a letter. We had another storm and almost hit an iceberg. We see more and more of them every day, so we must be getting closer to the North Pole.

This afternoon we sailed past a small penguin colony. They really are the most amusing creatures. I have done a drawing of them for you.

I went up to see the captain. He said that he could smell dry land. I was very excited by this, and I even tried to see if I could smell it too . . . but all I could smell were the kippers that Roo was cooking in the galley.

We had a very enjoyable meal tonight, and afterwards the captain told us old sea tales, some of which I found very unpleasant. Roo added a few of her grandfather's which I must say are becoming more and more ridiculous. She told us one in which he was swallowed by a whale and lived inside it for two years. He even built a little house in there, she said. He at last escaped by climbing out of the blow-hole, and swam all the way back to his ship. He got a medal for it.

Then Roo began another story about how he captured a pirate ship on his own. I went to bed.

If the captain can really smell land then we must be nearly there. I shall send this letter as soon as I arrive. Can hardly sleep tonight. Too excited.

With love,

your Grandfather.

My dear Child,

Hurrah! We have landed at Walrus Bay. The captain wished me luck and we shook hands. He gave Roo a tin of macaroni cheese. I think he really liked her. We were sad to see him go.

The town of Walrus is not a bad place really. There are a few shops, and a mailing station where I can send and receive letters. We went immediately to the mailing station to see if there were any letters for me.

Got a postcard from your Uncle Vincent in Australia, who went off looking for gold. It said:

WALLAMAGOO.
DUST VALLEY.
AUSTRALIA

DEAR BROTHER,
NO GOLD YET, BUT WHEN I
FIND SOME I WILL BE RICH.
AS IT IS I AM VERY POOR.
PLEASE SEND ME SOME MONEY.
LOVE VINCENT.

P.S. I HOPE YOU FIND THE POLAR BEARS OR
WHATEVER IT IS YOU ARE LOOKING FOR.

9c

WALLAMAGOO
10·9·97
AUSTRALIA

BLAST!

I sent him five pounds and a pair of my best golfing socks. I picked up the key to our new cabin and then we went to a shop called the Freezer Centre and bought some provisions.

Our cabin stands on a hill just outside Walrus. It was very dirty inside and seemed quite gloomy, but we soon cleaned it up and lit the stove. It has a bed, three chairs and a table, and a small shed outside for storing wood. It's not much, but it's home.

Very tired. Will write to you tomorrow. Tell your mother that I forgot to pack my woolly hat. Could she send it on to Walrus Bay for me. The address is:

> The Mailing Station
> Wolf Street
> Walrus
> Walrus Bay
> Nr. The North Pole

With love,

your Grandfather.

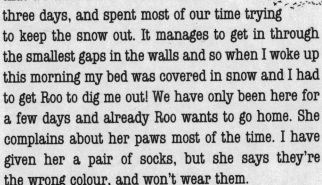

Dear Child,

I am sorry that I have not
written to you sooner. The
weather has been so bad
that we were stuck in the cabin for
three days, and spent most of our time trying
to keep the snow out. It manages to get in through
the smallest gaps in the walls and so when I woke up
this morning my bed was covered in snow and I had
to get Roo to dig me out! We have only been here for
a few days and already Roo wants to go home. She
complains about her paws most of the time. I have
given her a pair of socks, but she says they're
the wrong colour, and won't wear them.

Rather relieved when she went to bed, I'm afraid. I
should like to begin the long journey up to Great Bear
Ridge, but I don't feel that Roo is ready yet. She will
take more training than I thought.

Feeling a little low tonight.

With love,

your Grandfather.

Dear Child,

This morning I was woken by wolves running across my roof. It was the second time this week, and I must say I am heartily sick of it!

Roo says if they do it again she will leave. Where she thinks she will go I have no idea. Whether we like it or not we are stuck here and there is nothing we can do to change it. 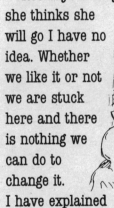 I have explained to Roo the purpose of our expedition, but she has a very short attention span and an even shorter memory. I must have told her a hundred times that we are looking for the Last Polar Bears.

Went down to Walrus this afternoon to stock up on provisions. We payed a visit to the mailing station and bought a pair of wellingtons and some blankets. Then

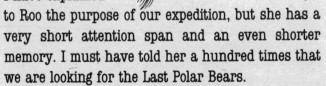

37

we went down to the Last Store and came out with a lot of things that we hadn't needed when we went in. That's what it's like in the Last Store. You just can't seem to stop shopping.

I bought an egg-timer, a jar of treacle, six Get Well cards, a stretcher, a footstool, a packet of jam labels and a puncture repair kit.

Roo's picture of the Rabbit.

Roo bought a very crude painting of a rabbit. Placed everything on the stretcher and dragged it back home.

Tomorrow we will attempt to go beyond Wolf Point. Tell your mother I have plenty of clean socks and there is nothing to worry about.

Wolves very restless tonight.

your Grandfather —

The Wolf Shed — I could not see a door.
I suppose they use the windows — Typical!

Dear Child,

This morning I found some wolves in my wood-shed
looking for dried fish. I told them I didn't have any
and they went away, but came back later with their
brothers and sisters and stole two pillowcases off the
washing-line and chewed holes in my new welling-
tons.

Repaired my boots with the puncture repair kit
and set off for Wolf Point just after lunch. Expedition
delayed as Roo refused to go past the wolves' shed.
They were lying in there with my pillowcases, and I'm
sure they had been drinking Old Sock because they
were singing. What a racket!
Roo was as bad though,
and even if she didn't
want to go past them,
that didn't stop her
from barking at them and
causing a general fuss. Several wolves
came out of the shed for a fight and Roo promptly ran
away, leaving me to deal with them. They were so
drunk by this time that they began to fight amongst
themselves and I left them to it. All this is Grogman's
fault. He shouldn't sell them drink.

Eventually found Roo again and harnessed her up to the trolley. My wellingtons leaked the whole way up to Wolf Point. The snow up here is very slushy from where the ice-caps have melted, and I'm sure the polar bears must be further up, where the snow is firmer. I think that they have gone up to Great Bear Ridge. If they're not there I don't know where they will be. Turned around at three o'clock and went back down the glacier towards the cabin. Went past the wolves' shed, but they were asleep.

Roo made supper tonight so I am feeling rather unwell now. It was a dreadful affair that consisted of last night's left-overs and something that had five legs and was very hard to chew.

Tell your mother that I am fine. I am seventy-eight years old and I can look after myself.

Your Grandfather

Roo and Snowmouse.
Roo is wearing cardigan that Uncle Freddie gave me for Christmas.

Dear Child,

One of my gloves is missing, so writing this is hard as I have to keep stopping to warm my hand. More trouble last night. A group of wolves arrived at my door past midnight and demanded to come in and see if we had any dried meat hidden away. I told them to go to bed, but I know that they went down to Grogman's and bought more Old Sock. They sang all night and I don't think I slept a wink.

This morning I got out the map and tried to work out a new route up to Great Bear Ridge. Wolf Point is too steep for Roo to pull the trolley up. The Narrow Valley is too narrow, and Windy Corner is too windy. I found a route called the Gentle Slopes, and decided that sounded most suitable.

In the afternoon we went to see my new friend Jackson, the snow poet. Jackson makes the most fantastic snow sculptures I have ever seen. At the moment he is working on a giant moose made entirely from snow and nothing else. When I arrived he was working on the antlers. Jackson has been here for a long time. He lives very simply and I often wonder how he manages at all. Nobody pays him to make the snow sculptures.

Jackson told me that the snow has begun to melt at Blue Whale Bay. He said he had been there on Monday and the sculpture of an albatross he made the week before had melted into the sea.

Before I left he gave me one of his snow poems as a present. It was printed on a block of ice. Jackson has written hundreds of poems about the snow, but this one I found very sad.

It went:

Oh snow, snow, snow,
when you melt,
where
do you go?

I do not knows
where melted snow goes.

I gave him two dried fish and a tin of toffees, then we said goodbye and went home.

I cooked tonight.

ICE, WATER AND STEAM,
ARE (NOT) THE SAME,
THOUGH YOU FIND FISH IN ALL OF THEM,
AND ALSO IN FLAME.
—JACKSON

Tell your mother I forgot to take my books back to the library and could she do it, please. It is snowing. The wolves are very quiet tonight.

Sweet dreams, Child.

your Grandfather.

My dear Child,

Very restless tonight. Roo will not
sleep in her basket and keeps getting into
my bed in the middle of the night. I wouldn't mind so
much if she didn't fidget and poke me with her paws.
Got up at five o'clock and made some tea whilst Roo
slept on in comfort.

This morning went down to the mailing station to
see if any letters had arrived for me. Got a letter from
your Uncle Freddie asking for his golf trolley back. I
am still using the trolley
to carry all our equipment,
so he can't have it back yet.

Sent him a telegram:

TROLLEY ACCIDENTALLY EATEN BY WOLVES.

Stopped off at the Freezer Centre and bought a jar
of toffees to keep my strength up. Of late I have found
I've been getting far too tired. It must be the cold.

Ate the toffees and felt refreshed. When I got back
it was eleven o'clock, and Roo was still in bed. How

can I head an expedition when my lead dog won't get up in the morning?

This afternoon there was an avalanche and a lot of snow fell from Wolf Point down into the valley. It is too dangerous to attempt to get up to Bear Ridge at the moment. The snow is melting more every day and this was the third avalanche this week.

As I write this letter to you Roo is cooking the dinner. The wolves have just gone past my window and one of them threw a snowball. The stove is throwing out a cheerful light and we are warm and safe. Do not worry about us, Child. Although Roo and I have never been on an expedition before, we know what we are doing.

Tell your mother that I am eating three times a day and always wear my scarf outside. I'm afraid I shall have to stop now, Child, as Roo says dinner is ready.

your Grandfather.

Dear Child,

How the wind howled last night! I thought it would blow the roof off our cabin. I did not sleep well. Melted some snow and made a pot of tea. It is very cold today and I fear that I am running out of time. I need to get up to Bear Ridge soon.

After breakfast I decided to pay Jackson a visit, to see how he was getting along with his snow moose sculpture. He was not very happy when I found him. The snow moose had melted. It looked more like a mousse than a moose. Only the antlers remained and they were melting too. I gave Jackson some oranges and a teapot to cheer him up, but as I made my way back down the hill, I'm sure I heard him weeping.

After a lunch of smoked cheese I took Roo to practise dragging the trolley, in preparation for our expedition. I played a little golf to keep my spirits up. I find that if I hit a good shot in the direction we are walking, the distance we walk to find my golf ball distracts us from noticing how far we have walked. I had to paint the balls red, so that they would show up against the snow. I've only got three golf-clubs with me: a driver for those long shots across the snow valleys, a five-iron for those medium shots across crevasses, and my putter for those delicate shots across the ice.

Roo does not like me playing golf. She does not watch me hit the ball and neither does she help me find it.

I had just played a particularly difficult shot over a small glacier (it was only thirty metres high, which is quite small for a glacier), when she decided she wanted to go home. She took off down the hill, dragging my trolley behind her and managed to tip it over. Golf balls, tent-pegs, tins of food, my driver and my beloved putter all came spilling out of the golf-bag and shot down a very deep ravine.

They are lost for ever.

Perhaps, a thousand years from now, they will be found, frozen solid into the ice, and scientists will argue over what they are. I am very angry with Roo tonight and have not spoken to her all evening. Wind only howling a little.

No sign of the wolves.

My love to your mother.

your Grandfather.

Dear Child,

I haven't been able to write to you for a few
days as we have had a terrible snowstorm. It
lasted for two days, and I have been cooped up in
here with Roo, unable to get out. I read to her from
a book called *David Copperfield*, but she said it had
no pictures of rabbits in it, so it was of no interest
to her.

She spent most of the time staring out the window,
though there was nothing to see, only the whirling
snow.

We ran very short on fuel during the storm, so I
had to burn some of our possessions to keep warm.

I burnt two chairs, two legs off the table, and Roo's
basket. If the blizzard hadn't stopped I would have
started on the floorboards.

Roo was very upset about her basket. She said she
was going to keep things in it. I said it was a pity she
hadn't slept in it.

In the end I had to tell her the story of the ice-
cream on Bear Ridge to cheer her up.
Once upon a time, I told her, the snow
was so pure and clean that it tasted
better than the finest ice-cream

money could buy. But as the air got dirtier from all the chemicals and fumes, the snow lost its taste. The last of the world's ice-cream lies up on Bear Ridge. Piles of it. And that's why we are going up to Bear Ridge. To get ice-cream for Roo. Roo loves to hear this story, though she has heard it many times, and I must admit that I have added bits – the fabulous chocolate mint chip, for instance, that can only be found in the shade, or the delicious strawberry split, found only at sunset. These are my own inventions.

Roo felt much better after this, and seemed keen to get up to Bear Ridge as soon as possible, to find ice-cream.

Dug our way out this afternoon and went down to Walrus to stock up on provisions. Spent a long time searching for the shops, as everything lay buried deep beneath the snow. Eventually found the mailing station after Roo fell down the chimney. Must have walked right across the roof. Roo wasn't hurt. However, she is now a black dog, rather than a yellow one. Everyone in the mailing station was much amused by this and someone even called her the Father Christmas dog, which got even more laughter. Roo went and lay beneath the counter and wouldn't come out.

I bought potatoes, porridge, oats, dried fish, tent-pegs and new welling-tons, and then discovered that the mailing clerk had a parcel for me. Your father had sent me my old one-iron, which I, in my haste to pack, had forgotten. I was extremely cheered by this and bought Roo a yellow ball, a scarf with flowers on it and a packet of roasted peanuts as a celebration. My one-iron is my favourite golf-club. It is not only good for long shots and putting, but is also an excellent ice-pick and walking-stick rolled into one. I am sure that with my one-iron I will now definitely make it to Bear Ridge and find the polar bears.

We walked past Grogman's on our way home, and I'm afraid it rather ruined our good cheer. There were several wolves hanging around outside drinking Old Sock, and as we went past they sang a very rude song about us. It went something like this, but I've taken the rudest bits out, as your mother wouldn't like it:

There was an old man and a little dog,
Yo-ho-ho and a bottle of Sock,
He was too mean to give us grog,
Yo-ho-ho and a bottle of Sock!

A poor brave wolf went to his door,
Yo-ho-ho and a bottle of Sock,
The old man booted him to the floor,
Yo-ho-ho and a bottle of Sock!

This is, of course, complete nonsense. I have never booted *anything* to the floor, let alone a wolf.

Snowballs were then thrown at us, but I ordered Roo to ignore them, and we got back home without further incident.

A fine meal of roast potatoes this evening. Roo did not eat much. I am sure that she has her own food hidden away somewhere in here. She is very careful with her money, and although I only give her five pence a week (which I think is plenty enough for a small dog), I am certain that she has more money than I do, and possibly more food.

Wolves got back very late from Grogman's, and sang another sixteen verses of the song on my roof.

Must go to sleep now. Very tired. Sleep well, Child.

your Grandfather.

Dear Child,

Woken this morning by wolves in my cabin. They had one of my pillowcases, and they wanted to trade it for some of my dried fish. After realizing that I was not going to be bullied into parting with any of our provisions, they stole two gramophone records and a pair of braces, and fled. What use these will be to them I have no idea, for they have no record-player, and no trousers to hold up.

Later on, Roo and I went to look for driftwood at Blue Whale Bay. Whilst we were gathering wood on the beach, some seagulls fell out of the sky, frozen solid. I packed them side by side, like a row of sardines, into my golf-bag, and took them home. I laid them by the stove, and a couple of hours later they had thawed out and come back to life. They were confused at first and flew round my cabin, knocking over books and smashing plates

Seagulls Thawing Out

and trying to fly through the windows to get outside. Eventually they calmed down, sat in a huddle on the floor and began to preen themselves. After they had thoroughly rearranged their feathers they became hungry, and waddled about the cabin looking for food. They were very hungry. They found the dried fish and ate the lot. They didn't like porridge oats, so they left that, but they finished off the rest of the potatoes and the beans. They found Roo's roasted peanuts, fought over them, and then polished them off. One even tried to eat the packet.

So now, as I write this to you, they are sleeping at last. Roo has just made some porridge, and I think after we have eaten we shall have an early night. We have no choice really, as one of the seagulls has broken my lantern, and it is getting too dark to see.

Good night, Child.

your Grandfather.

Dear Child,

The seagulls went on their way this morning. They left behind a terrible mess. Broken plates and dishes strewn across the floor, and everything covered in white feathers and bird poo.

Roo found the whole incident most distressing and said that I should have left them where I'd found them. We spent the morning tidying up after them. I can always tell when Roo is in a bad mood, because she constantly follows me with her broom and asks me to move. No matter where I went, that was where she wanted to sweep next.

She followed me all around the cabin, pushing a big pile of feathers and broken plates around with her broom. She wasn't picking it up, she was just pushing it from one side of the room to the other.

I decided to get out my one-iron and go golfing along the snow fairway. It is a difficult course to play. There are two crevasses on each side of the course, and if you hit your ball into them, it is lost for ever. At the end of the snow fairway there is a red flag that marks where the hole is. You have to get your ball into the hole in as few strokes as possible. Unfortunately there is nobody I can play golf with here. Roo does not like golf and Jackson does not see the point of whacking a ball about in the snow. So I play on my own.

My first shot went in the sea. The second went down one of the crevasses. As I am running low on golf balls I decided to play just one last ball before I packed in. I took my aim at the red flag, kept my eye on the ball, and gave it a mighty thwack with the one-iron.

The ball rose high into the blue sky, hung still for a moment as if deciding what to do next, and then fell in a graceful arc, out of sight beyond the crevasses. It was a magnificent shot and I set off after it immediately, to play the next.

I went carefully past the crevasses, because if you fall down there you're a goner. Then, in the distance ahead, I spied a small black shape, lying in the snow.

As I got closer I realized that it was a little penguin, unconscious, but still alive. Beside it lay my golf ball.

I wrapped the penguin in my coat, zipped it up in my golf-bag, and set off back to the cabin as quickly as I could. I laid it by the stove in a cardboard box. I feel very guilty about the affair and pray that it gets better. Roo and I had an argument when we went down to Walrus to buy more food. She said why didn't I invite the whole of the Arctic into our home and be done with it. We could fill the place with sea-lions, Arctic foxes and sea-birds, she said, and sleep outside. I had to tell her to be a little more caring for her fellow animals. She said they didn't care for her so she wasn't going to care for them.

Penguin still unconscious.

Tell your mother that I am well. I have thrown away the pills Doctor Strangler gave me and feel better without them.

A full moon tonight, and many stars. The stars seem to shine brighter here in the Arctic. Jackson says it is because the air is cleaner. You could see all the way across the valley, right up to Bear Ridge. It was like daylight, only more blue.

The wolves howled all night. A melancholy sound, lonelier than anything I have ever heard in my life.

your Grandfather

Dear Child,

Hip hip hurrah, and three cheers! The little penguin has woken up! It has a slight bump on its head, but apart from that is perfectly well. It ate six dried fish for breakfast and went back to sleep.

Went outside to get wood for the stove and it struck me that something was wrong. At first I could not make up my mind what was wrong. Then I noticed the sky.

One half of it was a deep blue and the other was a bright yellow. But even stranger than that was the sun and the moon.

They were side by side!

The sun had risen, as it always does, but the moon hadn't gone where it normally goes during the day. It had stayed.

I rushed back into the cabin and then I noticed the calendar. It said that today was the thirty-second of October, which can't be right as October has only thirty-one days, and today should be the first of November. Told Roo, and *she* said that she couldn't care less how many days there were supposed to be in October – every day was the same to her, and days shouldn't have numbers attached to them anyway.

Something very strange is happening though, despite what Roo says. I think we should set off as soon as possible for Bear Ridge, before it gets any stranger.

I started to pack immediately. Sent Roo down to the mailing station with a list of all the things we needed. She came back an hour later and said most of the food had gone. It seems as if everyone is leaving. Cannot decide what to do with the penguin. I feel responsible for him, but he does eat an awful lot of food. I cannot leave him here though. I shall take him with us until we find him a penguin colony to join.

Early night tonight. The wolves are very quiet. Tomorrow, come what may, we will head for Bear Ridge.

Do not worry about us, Child. We will be careful. I have my one-iron and I have Roo.

Sweet dreams.

your Grandfather.

A snowshoe Rabbit.

Dear Child:.

After harnessing Roo up to the trolley packed to the brim with food, tent, sleeping-bags, the portable stove and pots and pans, I closed the door to my cabin and we set off at once towards the Gentle Slopes. I did not look back in case I changed my mind.

We met the wolves on the way up to the slopes. I told them they could have my cabin and whatever else was left behind, but they shook their heads and said they were going north. One of them said something about the call of the wild. I found this as strange as the sky, which this morning was a pale green, and wondered what had happened to bring about such a change in them. For weeks they had lain around in their shack drinking Old Sock, and now suddenly they were making the difficult journey north. They ran across the snow towards Wolf Point, and then I lost sight of them.

They seemed different.

More like they must have been before the mailing station came.

Wolves.

Further up we met Jackson, at work on a giant walrus. I told him we were leaving for Bear Ridge. I gave him a few letters to post for us, thanked him, and we set off again. By lunch-time we had reached the Gentle Slopes and we started the long climb up.

Once I looked back and saw the cabin, a tiny speck in the distance, and it brought a lump to my throat.

Roo was pulling the trolley with great enthusiasm, no doubt driven along by the thought of ice-cream, and so by tea-time we were halfway up to the top.

We stopped and pitched the tent, crawled inside and lit the stove. After a large meal we got into our sleeping-bags. Penguin didn't, as he is used to sleeping without one.

By tomorrow we shall have reached the top. Very sleepy.

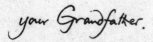

your Grandfather.

Dearest Child,

A terrible day! Whilst we were taking the tent-pegs out, a large gust of wind blew the tent away. We watched it float off over Blue Whale Bay. Fortunately I had taken the sleeping-bags out earlier or else it would have been a complete disaster.

We carried on up the Gentle Slopes. The wind started to blow harder. I tied us all to a piece of rope so that none of us would blow away. We made slow progress. At times Bear Ridge seemed to get closer and closer, but just as I thought we would reach it, it would get further away again. It must be like those mirages you get in the desert. The sky changed from lilac to a deep crimson and it started to snow.

We stopped and made an igloo, cutting out blocks of snow with my one-iron to make the walls. The wind grew more fierce, and we had just finished the igloo when the storm hit. It blew the trolley up into the air, taking Roo with it. I only just managed to catch one of the wheels with my golf-club and pull her back down. I grabbed her in my arms, undid the harness and the trolley flew off down the mountain.

Tonight we went through what we had left inside the igloo. We still have the stove, so we can cook, but we have very little food left. Just five fish and some porridge. That's all. Only one sleeping-bag. Everything else was in the trolley.

Very despondent tonight. I can hear the storm outside. Roo is wrapped up in the sleeping-bag. Penguin is asleep by my legs. When the storm is over we will walk up to Bear Ridge and everything will be fine.

I miss the wolves.

your Grandfather.

Dear Child,

The storm has not stopped. Poked our noses out to have a look and nearly had them blown away. The sky was as black as coal and the wind was moaning in a horrible way.

Stuck in the igloo all day. Played *I spy* with Roo, to keep her spirits up, but there were not many things in the igloo, so the game was very short. Shared out two of the fish and a little of the porridge between the three of us. The situation is grim.

Child, you know that I am old, don't you? That is one of the reasons why I went away. I have to see the polar bears before it is too late. The snow-caps are melting. The polar bears have nowhere else to go.

This is the last place on earth for them.

When I have seen them we shall come back. Don't worry, Child, we know what we're doing.

With love,

your Grandfather

Dear Child,

The storm has not stopped. We now have only three fish left and a little porridge. I read Roo the last chapter of *David Copperfield*, and then we burnt it.

How I long to get up and stretch my legs. But I know that if we went out in this storm, we would be lost for ever.

Too cold to write any more.

Perhaps tomorrow the storm will stop and we shall finish our journey.

Tell your mother that all is well. I don't want her to worry.

your Grandfather.

Dear Child,

We now have only one fish left.

your Grandfather.

Dear Child,

Thank heaven for Roo! This evening she produced a
tin of macaroni cheese, which she said she had been
saving for a special occasion. We all sat round the
little stove and watched it cook. It was the best thing I
have ever eaten!

Storm still going as strong as ever. All three of us
in sleeping-bag to keep warm.

Bless you, Child.

your Grandfather.

Dear Child,

Very weak, so this letter will be very short. We have no food left. The storm has stopped. In the wind I am sure that I hear voices. I thought I heard the wolves howling. The three of us huddled together.

Child, do not worry.

I know the polar bears will find us.

I feel more tired than I have ever felt in my life. I shall dream of the polar bears tonight.

Roo says she will dream about ice-cream.

Tell your mother that I will be home soon.

your Grandfather.

Dear Child,

The storm suddenly stopped and we all crawled out of the igloo. I only took my one-iron and a few golf balls with me. The sky wasn't purple or green, it was just blue.

We walked the last bit up to Bear Ridge under the warm sun. Penguin walked beside me, while Roo ran ahead, as dogs always do. At last we reached the top! Here I am, Child, on Great Bear Ridge, and it's like I dreamt it would be, only better. The wolves are here and I am happy to see them. The whales are here too, swimming amongst the icebergs. And there are penguins and seals. But most of all, the polar bears are here.

I can see them with their cubs, playing in the snow. I have not spoken to them yet, but I will.

Sleep tight, my Child. This is a beautiful world and it goes on for ever. I am tired now and must stop writing. Tell your mother that I love her.

Shush Roo. The polar bears are here.

Hush Roo. In the morning we will search for ice-cream for you.

Ice-cream for Roo.

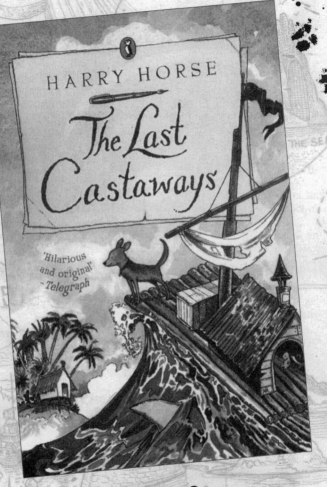